A Puppy Named Rufus

by
Professer Klunk

Illustrated by
Tina Lynch

Published by

**DOWN THE PATH
PUBLISHING**

First Edition
Published in Canada in 2009
by Down the Path Publishing
PO Box 344
Clearwater B.C. V0E 1N0
Email david@davidvanstone.com

CANADIAN CATALOGUING IN PUBLICATION DATA
Klunk, Clickity 1955-

A Puppy Named Rufus ©2009
by Down the Path Publishing
Illustrations ©2008 Tina Lynch

ISBN 13: 978-0-9689899-4-4

PRINTED IN CHINA

A Puppy Named Rufus

Now this is a story

About a dog who's not old,

A puppy named Rufus

Who didn't do as was told.

He lived in a house

Next to a forest on a hill

With two young children

Named Bianca and Gill.

They played in the yard,

Went for walks on a leash,

Although never into the forest,

Sometimes to the beach.

Then one day last summer

As leaves fell to the ground,

Rufus was left all alone

When the school bus came around.

Bianca and Gill told Rufus

At home you do stay;

When we get home from school

Then we will play.

But Rufus got lonely;

He sure missed those kids.

He didn't want to stay home,

So here's what he did.

After one hour

Of digging the ground,

The other side of the fence

Rufus now found.

He looked up the road

Which lead down to the beach;

Then heard from the forest

An interesting screech.

He ran into the forest

With a leap and a bound

Towards the owl who who

Who was making that sound.

He followed a path

In time to see

A busy little beaver

Dragging a tree.

Then barking and jumping

Into the mud just beyond,

As the beaver swam with the tree

To his house on the pond.

He saw a butterfly,

Heard the chirp of a cricket;

Then chased a quick rabbit

Into a thorny thick thicket.

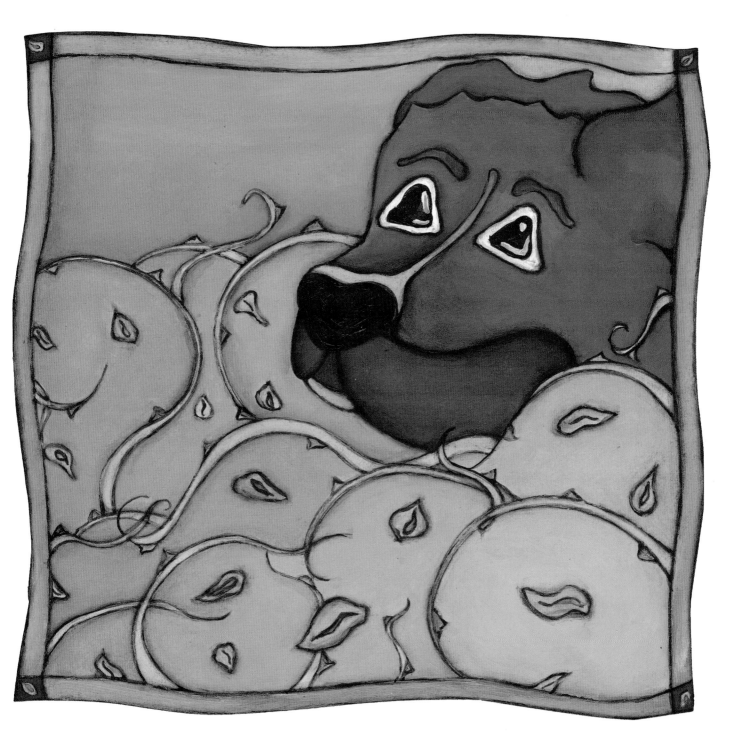

A family of raccoons

All ran up a tree;

He saw a 'possum looking at him,

Then two and now three.

Six pairs of red eyes

Were staring at him.

The day was now dusk

With the light getting dim.

Rufus was cold and hungry now,

Muddy, with burrs in his coat;

But, did Rufus know his way home?

The answer is nope.

He thought of the children,

How he hadn't done as was told;

If he had stayed home, he wouldn't be

Now lost, hungry and cold.

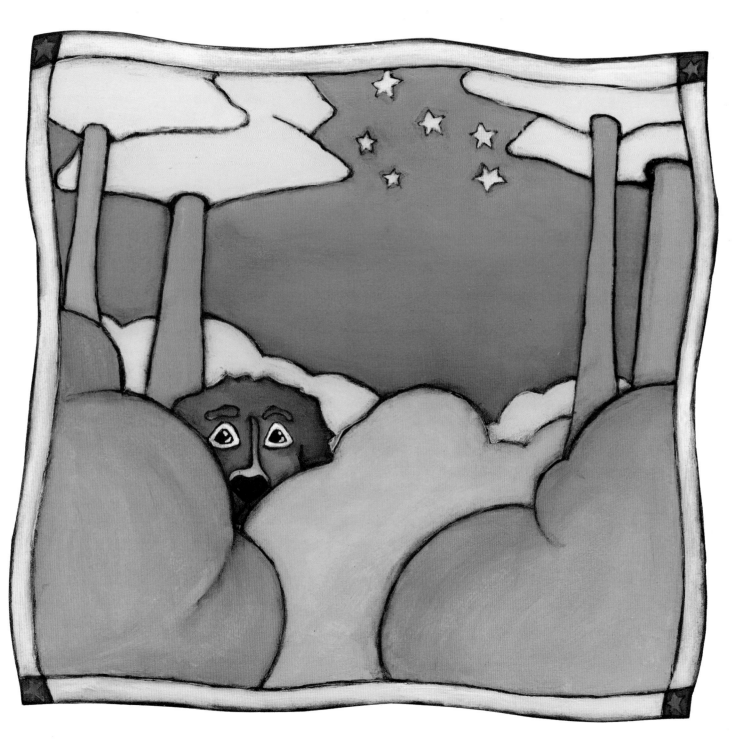

He could almost hear their voices.

He thought he could hear them again,

"Rufus, here Rufus" it was really real, yes!

Bianca and Gill were calling his name.

Rufus was oh, so happy

To be found at last!

And everyone felt better

After his bath.

So here ends this story

About a dog who's not old;

Rufus stays home now

Now without being told.

About the Artist

TINA LYNCH received her Bachelor of Fine Arts from the University of Victoria and she also has an Art Therapy Masters. She is lucky to live with her husband and two children on beautiful Gabriola Island, British Columbia. Her paintings have been exhibited in Victoria, Nanaimo and on Gabriola Island.

PHOTO BY LANCE SULLIVAN

Rufus was based on her dog Tyee, a charming Bernese Mountain Dog. Tyee spent most of his days on the beach, looking for treats, and bringing his toys to anyone passing by. The illustrations are a celebration of his life.

This is the first book Tina has illustrated and is looking forward to her next.

Proofread by Leslie Lindgrew and Helen Moller

Desktop Publishing by Linda Mullin
e-mail Linda@mullinart.com

This book is dedicated to
all the four-legged creatures
who chose to be our friends.

David Vanstone